The Fox
at Drummers'
Darkness

The Fox
at Drummers'
Darkness

JOYCE STRANGER

illustrated by William Geldart

A Carousel Book
Transworld Publishers Ltd.

THE FOX AT DRUMMERS' DARKNESS
A CAROUSEL BOOK   0 552   52159   0

First published in Great Britain in 1976

PRINTING HISTORY
Dent edition published 1976
Dent edition reprinted 1979
Carousel edition published 1982

Carousel Books are published by
Transworld Publishers Ltd.
Century House,
61–63 Uxbridge Road,
Ealing, London W.5.

Made and printed in United States of America
by Arcata Graphics, Buffalo, New York

Contents

1	Drumbeats	7
2	Hunger	14
3	Scavengers	25
4	Cats on the Prowl	35
5	The Old Huntsman	43
6	Johnny Toosmall	50
7	Drought	59
8	The Trap	66
9	The Phantom Army	71
10	Danger!	78
11	The Telltale	82
12	Green for Safety	91

Sharp on the air, a bonfire burning;
Crisp in the woods, the leaves red-turning;
Crack on the moors from the sportsmen gunning;
Quick through the fields, a red fox running.

To Bill Geldart
and by special request to
the children of Oyster Park
Middle School, Airedale, Yorkshire

1   Drumbeats

The red fox lay safe at Drummers' Darkness. Men never came there, and few beasts either.

They said in the village that, in the hours before the moon had risen, a man could hear the sound of drums. At first they came fast. *Drum, ta, ta, tum, Drrum tatatum. Drrum tatatum.* A triumphant army marching to battle, the pipes skirling, the swift flash and flourish of the merry drumsticks quickening the senses.

Then, just before dawn, when the stars paled to nowhere, drumbeats heralded the army returning from battle: slow and dead and sorrowful, terrifying the moor.

Behind them came the sound of running men, and softly the skirl of pipes. And when the men had passed, came the crying of women and children. Anyone near felt an icy rushing wind that fled across the grey spaces.

Yet, when day brightened, there was nothing. No mark of feet in the dew; no trace of the army that had tramped through the night. Nothing.

The moor was bleak as daybreak; was sour peaty soil, and dusty grey grass. It stretched to the horizon, unbroken by any human home. To the north it was marked by a little copse, a desolate place of close-growing, thin-trunked trees, where no flower ever showed in the soil beneath them and no bird ever sang in their branches. Even their leaves were sparse.

The wild beasts circled the copse. They circled the grey lichen-covered standing stones that marked its boundary. They circled the little granite headstone at the edge of the standing stones.

To the east and west of the moor were friendly woods, undercarpeted with flowers and grass, where birds sang. To the south was a farm, and the Huntsman's cottage and beyond these the distant town. A factory stood at its edge, chimneys soaring to the sky, belching smoke.

The fox found a den on the moor, close to the haunted copse, though he never went inside. Here, he knew, he was safe.

He was four years old, and he had never found a mate. He was long legged, lean flanked. His paws were black, his underbelly flushed with cream and the long fur on the rest of his body was a flaunting arrogant copper red, tainted with rust. Under his brush his long thick hairs were creamy white. His prick ears were black tipped, his glowing eyes were black rimmed, and his stiff whiskers were white.

He had been born in a thunderstorm, and the whole of his life since had been stormy. He learned, swiftly and terribly, that his chief enemies were men. Men, thundering on their stampeding horses, crashing over the ground, yelling and shouting, whips flailing, red mouths gaping as they shrieked yoick and tally-ho and yip, yip, yip, or their horns sounded the Gone Away or the Gone to Earth or the View-Halloo.

He knew that it was men who sent the racing hounds, the pack belling its bloodlust as it marked his trail, following his scent, running headlong on his track.

He knew that the hounds had torn his mother apart; he knew that men had come to the earth and sent down the terriers and pulled out his brother and two sisters and killed them too. He had been playing when the men came, and he had learned his lesson well. He froze, a red stone against the ground; a red pebble, a rounded rock, so still that nothing saw him and nothing scented him and the men went away, not knowing he was there.

He crept away that night, afraid to linger. There was blood-smell on the grass, fear-smell in the trees, and the thin drear rain that wetted him echoed his sorrow.

He was not very old and he was very lonely. He played with a stick, but it would not lie and pounce and bite and butt. He tried to play with a frog but it squealed and jumped into the water. He bruised his nose on the rolling hedgehog that armoured its body with spikes, hiding its soft parts from him.

He learned to hunt and he learned to kill. He learned that hounds could not track through water; they could not follow when his paws were soiled with cattle dung; they could not slide, as he could, through a narrow drain, and race down the hillside and leap into a tree. He lay along the branch, watching the hunt go by, and his scent blew into the air and away, never betraying his presence.

He knew where the geese fattened on the summer pools. He knew where the baby rabbits chased under the hunting moon. Night after night when he was full fed and comfortable and almost asleep, he lay with his nose on his paws and watched the moon running, speeding away from the shaggy grey cloud beasts as he ran from the pelting hounds.

He watched the trees dip and soar and creak and crash when the wind creature tore among them, lashing them with its fury, tearing small trees from the ground, flattening his fur with invisible fingers, taking the leaves and blowing them into his face, raising a duststorm that blew grit into his eyes so that he pawed them unhappily, making them even sorer than before.

He watched the river, learning that sometimes it was a thin trickle, a murmur of gentle sound as it spilled over the bedrock; and then at other times, when rain swept out of the sky and soaked the distant hills, the river became a ravening monster, raging in its bed, tearing at its banks, thrusting rocks and boulders aside as if they were pebble small. Twice in his life the angry water had spilled over the fields and the moors, drowning many farm animals and wild creatures. And then the fox fed well and was fat and thought the river his friend, so long as he did not fall into it and have

11

to wrestle with the urgent streaming current that forced everything before it as the water surged to the sea.

Night was his friend. Darkness that hid him when he hunted. Darkness that silenced the day so that he could creep unseen, without birds to shout his presence, to cry their warnings, to scream to one another. Fox. Fox. Fox.

At night men went to rest. At night the lights were dimmed. At night the day creatures slept, and were off their guard and he could creep up unseen. He needed silence. The deep stillness that was unbroken by manvoice or birdcall or dogbark. He moved like a shadow, nosing the wind. The steady wind, unveering, helped him in his hunting, hiding him behind it, so that it blew always towards his nose, stroking his fur flat, bringing him every whiff and taint and rumour of food.

His damp nose took the scent and his quick brain told him what was there. Frog in the drowning ditch, flooded by last night's rain. Hedgehog under a dock, hiding from him, its breathing noisy as he passed. Scent of rabbit, strong, mouth watering, tempting, as he stole softfoot onto the grass that hid the warren, creeping, belly close against the ground, scarcely stirring the grasses, barely shifting the flower tops, swiftly running towards the unsuspecting doe that was grooming its coat, unaware of danger.

The old buck at the corner of the warren caught a taint of foxsmell.

Thump on the ground.

Rabbits running.

Pounce and swift kill. The young doe was too slow. The fox ran off with the body in his mouth,

12

through the woods where the day was turning the slender trees to red, to brown, to black, to silver and to gold, avoiding the close packed trunks of the haunted coppice, over the dry grey grass, stirring the dead clumps of last year's seedheads, back to his lair on the haunted moor where he listened to the last faint ripple on the drums as the sun crept over the hill. He saw the army pass, and vanish in the little copse beyond his den.

The fox fed. He lay, curled in a ball and the drums sang softly. *Pip, pip, pip, a pip. Pit, pit, pit a-pit.*

Day was a full flood of light and colour. The wind stirred the grass and the drumbeats faded on the air. There was silence. These were his days and his nights and this was his home, on the desolate moor, where man, alive, never came, for fear of the dead.

2 Hunger

That summer was hot. The sun blazed daily from the clear blue sky; the grass was parched and sere; the streams dried to trickles. The wild beasts were starving. No grass to fatten the rabbits; and the fox fed sparsely too.

Hunger was his constant companion. Hunger was a gnawing ache from dusk to daybreak, and a raging pain from daybreak to nightfall. He ate roots. He ate fallen fruit in the orchards and suffered because it was not yet ripe. He lay, smelling the wind. The wind brought news of chickens and geese and ducks on the distant farm on the other side of the grey moor.

Fat chickens, plump and feathered, scratching in the dust. Big white geese smelling richly, mouth watering. He dreamed of geese, of chicken, of duck, of food filling his belly, easing the cramping pain, so that he could sleep through the day in the dimness of his dusty earth, away from the scorching sun that sucked the goodness from everything.

There had never been such a summer.

The sky had forgotten rain.

The leaves on the trees crackled in the small winds that blew at dusk, adding their faint stirrings to the never relenting drums.

Ssssssssssss . . . drrrrrum . . . drrrrrummm . . . drummmm.

The fox ached with hunger and watched the phantom army gather at twilight; he was aware of the change in the note of the drums and the faraway pipes. First the faint humming; then the call to arms and then the quick delight of the drummer beating as he marched at the head of the horde. They came from the little copse.

They came in a swirl of mist, filled with shapes; shapes of men and women and of small children, shapes of soldiers marching. Behind the drums was the heavy thump of many feet, and behind the noise of the marchers was the wail of women, soft and low, a shrill keening that sounded like the sigh of the wind over the heath.

The fox curled closer, nose to tail, and settled himself. He had more news of the fat birds that the farmer cosseted, knowing they were his lifeline. Even the milk was in short supply as the cows had only dry sun-burned grass on which to fatten. The farmer needed his birds to bring him money to tide him over until the rains came.

Rain.

Men prayed for it in the churches.

The flowers thirsted for it and wilted in the gardens.

15

The ground was iron hard.

The fox was afraid of the farmer. Once, he had visited the farm, crouched low, his eye on a chicken that had wandered too far from her sisters. The old man saw the flash of rusty fur and swore and loaded his gun. The red fox ran off with shot in his hind quarters. The wounds healed, but the pellets were there to this day. He had cause to remember.

Nothing moved by day on the moor. The blinding sun was too fierce and the beasts sought shade.

There was another curse that summer, worse than the curse of heat and drought.

There was a plague of insects.

Flies that buzzed and teased and tickled and tormented. Midges that hung in hordes on the air and stung so that skins itched and the tiny black horrors were trapped in dense fur, to sting, and sting and sting again.

The fox was not bothered in his earth, but he suffered when he came out at dusk. He sat and pawed at his nose and his smarting eyes, at the swarms stinging at his sensitive ears. He could not take refuge in water, though several times he rolled in the muddy centre of the biggest tarn to gain relief.

He could not bear the hunger.

He could not stand the flies.

And always, the wind told him of food at the farm; food in quantity. Food for the taking. Except for the old farmer and his gun.

The fox grew thin. His coat lost its richness. He was a mangy animal, dusty coated, ears and nose bleeding where he had scratched furiously to rid

16

himself of insects. His skin was tight on his ribs and he was weak with hunger.

One late June night the sun died in a surge of blood. The reddened sky faded. The twilight army came from the copse. The drums faded in the distance. The moor was very still.

Wind rustled the dry grass. A grasshopper sang its maddening song. A mouse rustled, squeaked and vanished into a hole. The fox was too slow in his pounce.

The wind strengthened, bringing the tang of farmbirds. A tang that started the saliva rolling in his mouth, that alerted his empty gut so that it griped for lack of food.

The sky had vanished. Darkness hid the world. There was a ghost moon low in the sky, beyond it one faint star. Light barely touched the moor. Shadows stretched all the way to the farm.

The fox left his earth.

He moved quietly, his paws barely marking the ground. He travelled slowly, cautiously, stopping often to listen. Silence. No hint of danger. No sound of man or beast, except for the far away unearthly call of a hunting owl.

Wait. One paw raised. Head alert. Ears moving, to and fro, listening. Analysing the darkness, wary for danger.

Danger that might crack from the darkened farm buildings. Danger, that might stem from the sharp bark of the guarding dog. Danger that might rise from the stamp and whinny of a horse, warning other creatures that here came the prowling fox, anxious to steal and kill.

Listen.

Move slowly, one paw, a second, a third, a fourth. Muscles clenched, ready to run. Pounding heart and tightened throat. Fear of sudden dying, of dying unmated. For that he had been born. His life lacked fulfilment and his instinct told him that he must stay alive and unharmed.

His instinct told him he must feed soon, or waste away, unable to gather strength to hunt.

Food was a driving need.

Food was a wild craving.

There was nothing left in his life but the desire to eat.

The farmer had built a new henhouse some distance from the main buildings of the farm. He was not a good carpenter, but labour was too expensive to hire and he had done his best. He had not done well. The forty hens were protected by wood and wire, but the wood had gaps and the nails had not bedded true.

The fox reached the henhouse.

The wind was a mere whisper. The moon had vanished from the sky. Above him was a vast vault, filled with glittering stars. Starlight was friendly.

The enemy was manlight, shining from the great bulked buildings in which the farmer lived. Tonight no telltale yellow patch broke the humped stone walls. Within the farmhouse, everyone slept.

The old farm dog had died.

There was a new puppy, as yet too young to guard. The pup whimpered, smelling fox, but he often whimpered with loneliness at night and the farmer threw his boot downstairs and yelled to him to shut up.

The fox heard the noise and crouched, heart

racing, close against the henhouse walls. The little wind helped him, blowing away his smell from the chickens, though it was blown towards the pup. The pup whined again.

The farmer shouted for silence.

The pup was afraid of his master and dared not call again. He could not understand why no one came. The smell of fox was rich on the air, drowning the scent of the farm kitchen; the scent of home-cured bacon hanging from hooks in the ceiling, of bunches of dried mint and sage and thyme, of strings of onions.

There was the leftover scent of the day's baking—crusty yellow bread, scones light as a swan's feather, a sponge cake rich with jam, and carefully gathered cream from the milk of the Jersey cow that was kept for the household, a piece of ham stuck with cloves and boiled with onion, and the dog's own meat scalded to make a broth to wet the biscuit.

There was the musty scent of the mice in the wainscot, coming from the hole where the tabby cat crouched, waiting, and the smell of old Tab herself, comforting and familiar, as she had adopted the pup when her kittens were drowned, as they always were. One would be allowed to survive from her litter when she was old, to replace her. Outside, the tom cats ranged, four of them, keeping down the rats, but they had all left home tonight and gone hunting the enticing scent of the ginger she-cat at the gamekeeper's cottage a mile down the road.

The memory of them too lay on the wind, but the smell of fox was stronger than any of these, coming in waves of rank musk. The pup had never smelled fox before, but he knew it meant danger.

Silence.

One minute stretched to ten, to twenty, to thirty.

A horse stamped restlessly, turned in its stable and settled to sleep. A cow mooed. There was a rumour of drums in the far distance. The farmer's wife woke and heard them, and crossed herself and said a prayer.

Hail Mary, Mother of God.

Fearsome things moved out on the moor.

There was a tree beyond the henhouse. Winter bare, stripped of bark, lightning tormented. Its twin branches speared towards the sky. From one of them spiked a long thin sparsely leafed twig and from the twig, hanging broken necked, was the body of a crow, swinging on the air.

The crow had taken a chick two days before. The farmer shot it and strung up the body to warn its fellows not to poach on his ground. One wing lifted in the breeze.

The fox saw the movement and crouched, petrified with fear. He knew that this was manmade death. The rope was almost a foot long and the bird hung, sinister.

The fox wanted to run away, away from the threat of the speaking stick that the two-legged beast carried; away from the telltale body of the crow.

He was too hungry.

The wind brought the chicken smell so that it poured over him, exciting him. He pawed at the wood. The nails came free and a plank leaned outwards.

He listened.

The stir of wind, the hint of drumbeats, the uneasy feel of the sleeping house, the almost unheard whine of the anxious pup, the breathing of cattle in the field, the heavy shuffle of the horse, the terrifying *pit* as one dry leaf fell from the tree, startling the night.

There was a faint chickering from the henhouse. The birds slept, head under wing. The wind was a traitor, telling them nothing.

Wait, lest another sound broke the stillness. Wait and be sure. Instinct was the fox's master. He had to take care. He had to beware.

He took the end of the plank in his mouth and dragged it away. He moved it cautiously, so that it slid over the dry ground almost noiselessly.

He squeezed through the gap.

A faint glim of light showed a bird beside him. He took it by the neck.

Wings flapped and panic clamoured, awakening the other birds. Noise, shouting to the world that here was a thief. Terrifying wings fluttering, birds flying in the darkness, beating against him, screeching their terror.

Inside the farmhouse the farmer swore viciously and grabbed his trousers and his double-barrelled shot gun. It was unloaded and he could not find the ammunition in the dark. There was no electricity. Only the soft glow of oil lamps, that needed to be found and primed. The candle in the candlestick by his bed had burned to a stump and refused him light.

In the henhouse the fox sprang and killed. Killed the hens that flapped and screeched and squawked and fluttered, by biting off each head with one swift furious snap. Snapping at peril that

21

threatened him and that destroyed his immunity. Snapping at the idiot birds that beat from side to side in the darkness.

Slowly, the noise grew less.

One after one, the birds died and with each death, there was lessening of the din, and fewer flailing wings to fly across his face, and hit against his aching hungry body.

Kill and kill again.

And at last, the bliss of utter silence.

Not a sound betrayed his presence. He seized the body nearest to the gap in the henhouse wall and slipped into the farmyard.

Over the wall and away.

The yells of fury followed him. The useless shot sped after him. The darkness befriended him.

He loped over the moor, and stopped near the dried up tarn to eat. Food at last. The warm flesh filled the aching cavern inside him, eased the agonizing cramps, brought strength.

He rested among the white feathers until just before daybreak.

He drank thirstily from the muddy trickle and went to his earth.

The telltale feathers fluttered on the moor for many days, recording his crime.

The farmer swore revenge.

The red fox slept, soothed by the sound of drums. The mist eddied and swirled on the moors and the voices cried in the rustling grass and in the ranked dry reeds at the margins of the pools.

Then came silence.

Far over the moors, beyond the farmhouse, a puff of cloud swirled across the blue and masked the sun.

The red fox slept on, full fed.

The farmer took the dead hens to market, selling them angrily. On his way home he stopped off at the cottage next door to the farm, and had a word with the old Huntsman who still kept hounds for his own pleasure though few men could now afford to hunt.

3   Scavengers

Years of watching men had taught the fox cunning. He knew where men walked by day, where they hunted in the autumn, where they sought the cubs. He had learned long ago that they never came near the haunted wood.

The nightly phantoms were a misty reminder of a long-ago past that the fox would never understand. He did understand that the ghostly horde sped by and never offered him harm. Men threatened him whenever they appeared; with gun and hound and baited trap; with poisoned rabbit carcasses that stank of their hands, and that he knew at once were tainted and left to lie. Sometimes the crows pecked at the flesh and died horribly.

The summer drought baked the earth rock hard.

The duck pond was only a memory. There was

nowhere for the birds to swim. The farmer's temper shortened daily. Water ran from the pipes in the house, but water had to be carried to the cattle in the fields, to the sheep at the edge of the moor, to the ducks and geese and the hens. His arms ached with lugging heavy buckets as the hose would not reach the fields and fill the troughs.

The oats in the planted fields were thin and spare; no profit there. The barley did not grow ears and fatten. The potatoes were not worth lifting from the ground. The fruit fell from the bushes long before it was ripe.

The price of feeding stuffs rose to astronomic heights.

Beasts were killed. There was no money to buy feed for them.

As summer progressed the sound of the drums grew louder night by night. The farmer knew that this meant disaster. The Huntsman knew that ruin stared at all of them. He was an old man, his mind not always clear, so that at times he took his coppery nag and his hounds and hunted imaginary foxes over the fields, at the wrong time of year, forgetting what was right and what was wrong.

The children feared him almost as much as they feared the smoke-haze armies that marched in the morning mist. Their elders told them the tales. He galloped through the villages, his mellow horn blowing loudly, his struggling hounds, long past their prime, panting as they kept up with the bony horse that should have been retired long ago.

The children were not sure that he too was not a ghost.

The Huntsman was old. He knew all about the armies. His great-great grandfather had been one

26

of the marching men, and had left his body and his blood on the far-away hills, and never come home to his lonely wife and his five small children. The Huntsman's father had heard the tale from his father, who had it from his father too. The Huntsman's father remembered the stories vividly, and told his children how their ancestors had died, in a sweep of men with pikes who thrust through the breaking ranks, yelling like demons.

There had been tears in the village for many months after that battle. Sometimes the old man thought his cottage walls must still be wet with tears that were shed at that time. He often sat on the porch, swinging to and fro in the rocking-chair that must have seen that first night's weeping, so long ago, thinking of the battle and of what might have been if the army had won, and the invaders driven from the land. He had forgotten they were not strangers now, but men with whom he had worked and lived and hunted over the fields and woods.

He would never hunt the moor. There were too many tales.

The fox knew the Huntsman well; knew his savage face, his staring eyes, his yelling mouth; knew how he whipped his horse and called the hounds to the kill. Man was the only enemy.

The season was wrong for hunting. The Huntsman was having one of his rare, lucid periods and refused to go out after the fox till the autumn. It would have to wait.

The farmer cleaned his gun. He sat, night after night, at the window, swearing at his wife when she begged him to rest, to come to bed, to ease his anger which was mastering him, making him hot tempered, unbearable to live with, so that she went about her work with a closed and anxious face. The outdoor cats fled when the farmer crossed the yard and the pup did not dare a bark or whine, but crept under the kitchen table, hiding himself under the long red plush cloth, bobble edged, which always covered it and made a dark and secret place where he and the cat could take refuge until the man went outside again.

The fox knew better than to return.

He was so hungry that he wandered widely, and for the first time in his life visited the place at the edge of the moor.

A vast factory complex had grown here, sprawling along the edge of the hill. Chimneys towered into the sky, blackening the day with billowing smoke. Here, at the very edge of the moor, grass was stunted; the wild flowers had died long ago; the ground was blasted, bare and black with soot. The river ran shallow and foul, a stinking ribbon patched with flecks of foam, and dead fish floated, bodies glistening with decay.

Any beast that drank the water died.

The sour soil hurt the fox's paws. He paused and licked, and was suddenly and swiftly sick.

He skirted the ground, finding a hard path that led away from the factory into the heart of the town. Men were asleep. The glowing street lamps showed nothing but the fox's shadow, growing eerily long, shrinking uncannily, fading, and reappearing on the opposite side of him, worrying him. He was used to sun shadow and moon shadow, predictable as dusk and starset, but he had never seen ranked lamps before, nor watched the change as he ran between them.

At first, as the shadow flashed along the ground, he froze, watching the unnerving shape freeze with him. Then, as he ran, it began to play again, first large, then small, a fleeting silent darkness glued to his paws by a magic that he never understood.

A cat sped in front of him, turned, horrified, and swiftly slashed his face in quick daring. It knew the free ways better than he, so that it leaped, lightning fast, over a wall and vanished under a garden shed, leaving him, nose bleeding, shaking his head to clear his mind, unable to understand what had attacked him and then vanished so swiftly.

He came to a row of shops.

He stood, puzzled. Here there was no grass, no water, no trees. Nothing was familiar. The overpowering terror-inspiring stench of man and his affairs drowned all natural smells except the markings left around the lamp-posts by a colony of dogs.

He sniffed.

A bitch in season.

Dogs of all kinds, big and small. He added his own mark, a musky reeking tang that would drive every dog in the town mad next day, and plodded on, drawn by the foodsmells that hung on the air.

The memory of the day's frying hung on the air all around the chip shop, so that saliva rose in his mouth and flooded his throat, choking him. He stopped to cough, the hunger ache masking caution.

The chip shop was closed and shuttered. Here the smell of man was so strong that the fox almost turned and fled to the moor again, but there was no food on the moor and there was food here.

He listened, head up, seeking news on the wind, paw raised, ready to run, every muscle taut.

The only sound was the far away drone of an engine across the sky. He lifted his head, pinpointed the noise, and watched the giant eyes blink on and off. No danger there. The winking lights vanished always and never came down to threaten him. He had seen many planes.

He crept over the pavement.

No lights in the windows. No footsteps in the streets. No movement.

Pause, to listen.

Creep again.

He moved as silently as his own shadow, not a sound to alert a listener, not a movement that would catch the eye. Past the shop window, now hidden by a blind that made a mirror-like surface, reflecting him.

He turned his head.

Another fox.

He snarled. The enemy snarled back. He butted and hurt his nose on hardness. There was no scent or feel of fur. He backed away, growling, and the enemy fox backed too. No point to fighting. There was nothing there.

Bewildered, he crept on, past an arched doorway, shying at an empty milk bottle. It was washed and clean and smelled of soap, not milk.

There was a dark alleyway between the shops.

From here came the call of food.

The fox slipped over the flagged pavement, bruising his sore pads against uneven edges. He crept, even more slowly, hearing a scurry and rustle. He lifted his head.

30

Rats!

There was a strike in the town, and no bins had been emptied for three weeks. The rubbish spilled around them, in stinking mounds, and among the mounds were brown backs and long tails and sharp snouts, as the rats burrowed, feeding rich. They were sleek and fat, and their sharp teeth were vicious. Black eyes glittered, reflecting the gleam from the street lamps.

The fox smelled fish.

The rats had swarmed onto the bins, pushing under the half lifted lids, which could not bed evenly on the overflowing rubbish. They had brought down everything that was edible, leaving it on the ground, amongst paper greasy with the tag ends of chips, and endless peelings and bones, and heads and tails.

The smell was overpowering.

The fox picked at a fish head and ate a few cold stale chips. Then, seeing a rat scurry close to him, unable to smell him because of the overpowering odours of the bins, he crept forward on bent legs, his tail sweeping the dust, and pounced.

The rat was an old rat and wily.

He twisted and bit.

The fox let go, his lip bleeding. The rat, bleeding too, crept into the piled rubbish and hid.

The fox had no urge to hunt him further. He prowled among the bins, taking food from first this one and then that. He found rich trophy a little farther along where a butcher had flung out a few meaty bones for the dog.

The dog was chained in his kennel, fast asleep.

The wind blew his scent to the fox, who knew that it was safe to venture near.

He crept, slowly, slowly, towards the biggest

bone, a hugh marrow bone, rich and meaty, the meat still fresh. Suet clung to it, shining in the light of the lamp that overlooked the yard. The fence here was very low, a token fence, no problem for the fox.

He leaped the fence, snatched the bone and ran, over the fence again, down the alleyway, his paws whispering over the cobbles, the rich flavoured meat welcome in his mouth. The dog scented him, woke and barked, but no one heard. The shops were deserted at night, the dog left alone, a warning to intruders.

The fox raced along the streets. He was now used to his weirdly behaving shadow. He loped over the fouled ground and back onto the moor, as the moon fell out of the sky and the sun glinted behind the mountains, giant bulks blocking the horizon.

The armies were returning, a tired rabble, the drumbeats faltering, the children weeping, the women wailing, the men plodding in disarray, after their nightly defeat.

The fox ran between them, through the rising mist that teased at his fur and damped it, and out again onto the edge of the moor to take the well-trodden path to his earth, there to still his panting breath and quieten his thudding heart. He gnawed noisily at the meaty bone, until not a shred of flesh remained on it, and his sharp teeth had cut away the bone itself and torn out the marrow.

Splinters of bone whitened the ground around him.

The last pit of the drums had long since died. The sun blazed over the moor.

33

The Huntsman woke, whistled his dogs and saddled his horse, and then remembered he had not eaten. He left the nag standing in the sun, head hanging, reins tied to a bush. He fed the dogs and brought food for the horse, and cut himself a slice of bread to toast, but forgot to toast it. He took it outside and ate it without butter or jam, and thought the horse looked hot. He brought water and took the animal indoors to the darkened stable again. He removed the saddle and laid it carefully across his bath, unable to remember where he usually kept it.

His white moustache blew out as he talked to himself, reminding himself of jobs to do, and of a fox to be hunted for the farmer down the road.

His cracked voice sang out.

'D'ye ken John Peel,
With his coat so grey?'

The words echoed on the dry moor. Far away, the fox heard them, and curled in his dusty pen, knowing the Huntsman's voice, and fearing that it would be followed by the long call of the horn and the wild belling of the pack.

The wind rose.

The trees rustled.

The dry dust blew into the mouth of the earth.

The fox turned his back on the entrance, buried his nose in his dust covered fur and slept wearily, one ear always listening for the call of the blackbird in the spiked dead tree, warning him of danger.

4 Cats on the Prowl

Day succeeded dreadful day.

The newspapers reported the drought—the worst on record. Cattle suffered as the grass could not grow without rain. The sheep fared better as they were used to sparse feeding, but they too were thin.

The stream was a rusty trickle between the banks. The dry stones were too hot for the fox to walk on. His pads had not recovered from the chemicals at the edge of the moor. They had skinned and were sore: he dared not lick them. He walked painfully, his swift slip and slide a memory, as he limped by night, always conscious of hunger and thirst.

One night he loped, lagleg, over the moor, drawn by the smell of water. He lapped from the sheep trough, but the sheep scented him and deafened the night with their panic bleats and calls.

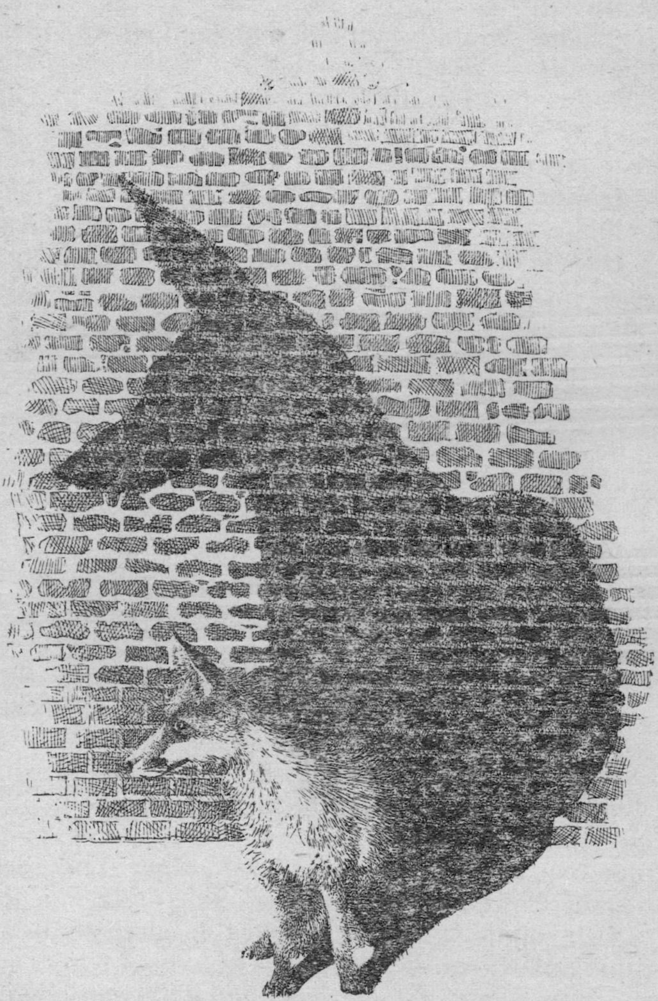

The lights flashed on in the farmhouse. The door was flung wide and patterned shadows dappled the yard.

The booted steps thundered, shaking the ground.

Tramp. Tramp. Tramp.

The fox ran.

His paws hurt and he was slow. The moon betrayed him, shining on his bushy tail. He was no longer red, but grey, grey with the dust and grit that he could neither lick not wash from himself. The crack of the gun sent him speeding into the heather, the dust rising behind him as the shot hit the ground. He forgot his sore paws and fled, darting between the bushes, breath panting, ribs lifting until the muscles ached.

Behind him came the high call of the farmer's wife and the man's steady angry cursing.

The sheep noise stilled.

The fox returned to the town, avoiding the paw-skinning grass, finding a new way that led through twisting alleys to the shops where there was now rich bounty. The smell of rotting food hung on the air, drifting through the streets and sometimes, when the wind came from the southeast, reached the moor.

He knew that where the food lay there would be young rats and good hunting.

He limped, but moved swiftly.

He had never seen so many rats. They came from every crack and cranny. The night was noisy with squeak and chitter and the harsh scratch of long claws on the uneven cobbles.

The rats swarmed over the bins, swarmed into the bins, nibbling at the rotting food, carrying it away in tiny sharp-fanged jaws, fighting over the meatier pieces. They strewed paper in which rubbish had been wrapped, so that the alleyways were filled with the dustbin leavings. The wind took the paper and blew it into the streets.

The fox found shelter in the angles of the walls, in the alleyways between the shops, in the empty doorways. Night after night he came, when the streets were empty of people, when the shops were shuttered, their blinds drawn; padding through the lonely streets, his shadow playing with the lamps. Sometimes his shadow was flung upon a wall, a giant fox, sharp jawed, ears dwarfing his head, twitching as he moved; the shadow arched as he pounced.

The town was his. No one walked through the darkness. Occasionally a police prowl car passed him, but the patrol men did not see the animal frozen in the blackness against the walls. Sometimes the headlamps illuminated the shine in his eyes, but the two men thought it revealed a cat, as many cats came to hunt among the teaming rats.

The fox learned to know them all. The slender tabby, her gentle face belying her skill, as she crouched, swayed, waited and then pounced, her teeth wicked. She learned to take the young rats, as yet unskilled at fighting.

There was a ginger tom, a weighty warrior, well over fourteen pounds of muscle and bone and sinew, swift to mark his prey, apt to hunt for the joy of hunting, for the watch, creep, pounce and play, jumping backwards away from the backlash twist and tease of tooth that threatened to maim him.

There were five black-and-white warriors, father

and four of his sons, each son born to a different she cat, who always came in a group and hunted with determination. The dead rats lay in the yards each morning, a revealing telltale to the men who found them there and who burned the bodies, sure there could be no more. Yet each day they were wrong. They never saw the swarms that came after dark, or the four-legged hunters that followed them, knowing where the feeding was rich.

The fox avoided the cats. His first encounter had been with the eldest son of the black-and-white tom, and he had no wish to risk another. The long raking claws had scarred his ear for life, slitting it at the end, so that he wore a badge that would point him out to any man that saw him, a frayed ear, with two points instead of one.

He was still lame. The chemicals had burned deep, and the pads were raw and skinned. But he had to find food, or die of slow starvation.

The cats and the fox and the rats raided night after night. Beyond the edge of town, the flare-offs from the factory chimneys would suddenly light the yards where the animals warred eerily, showing the skirmishes that raged, echoes of duels that men had fought over the moors.

The phantom army was here too. It fled through the factory which had been built on their old battleground. There, among the sheds, the tanks and the storage vats, there, among the offices, the steam pipes and the steepling chimneys, the drumbeat echoed. It mingled with the beat and click and thud of machinery, losing itself under the hiss of steam, re-appearing in the silences between the opening and closing of the clattering valves.

Druuum, drum, drrrrum.

Sss thump, sss thump . . . drrrrum.

Silent as the smoke that billowed from the chimneys, the battle was fought in the concrete yards and through the twisting maze of piping. Only the nightwatchman was there, and he was afraid that he laced his vigil from the whisky bottle to give him false courage. But the bottle addled his wits and fuddled his senses and stimulated his fears, so that soon he gave in his notice and then came another man, tempted by the high wages . . . and another. No one ever stayed more than a few weeks. The armies were invisible, but the dark night was dominated by fear. The nightmen felt unseen eyes watching them, saw shadows that should not exist, and heard the uneasy echoes of drums coming from the empty air.

Dawn gathered the fighting spectral shapes. They returned wearily to their hidden place in the wood. The mist that followed them hid the grass and bushes, drifted waisthigh on the air, and hid the fox that loped, full fed, back to his den in the side of the hill, under the roots of a long forgotten dead tree, that was only a memory above the earth.

The rats returned to the sewers; fled to the safety of the underground factory world, among the steam pipes where no one ever came and where their nurseries were warm and soft and undisturbed and they bred freely. Sometimes the rat catcher put down poison but these rats laughed at poison, fattening on the bait, totally immune to every trick devised by man.

The cats went home.

The little grey tabby returned to a tiny prettily furnished house at the edge of the town, mewing lovingly to her mistress. The old lady let her in, cuddled her close and offered her chicken and scrambled egg and other dainties. She often took her to the vet because she would not eat, never knowing that her gentle puss was a tiger by night, feeding full on rats and mice that left her without room for other dainties.

The black-and-white tom cats lived in the factory complex. Here they were encouraged by the men who knew there were rats underground, out of sight and out of reach. They found the rat droppings on the floors of the canteens; they found them in the offices, where men ate sandwiches and did not notice the dropped crumbs. The cats were on the payroll; their food was scarce, as they were kept as hunters, but the men brought them titbits; shared sardine sandwiches with them, and bits of fried fish from the chip shop, and always, each had a saucer of milk.

The men had named them too.

Buster and Bouncer. Bludgeon and Brainstorm and Bobby One-eye, who had lost his eye long ago, when he was only a kitten, without enough sense to realize he wasn't big enough to tackle a rat. One of the men had seen the fight and killed the rat with a mighty blow from an iron bar and taken the kitten to the vet and tended him at his home in the terraced street beyond the shops. Bobby One-eye always came to greet the man who had nursed him and was always rewarded with a piece of chocolate sponge cake, filled with cream, that he loved even more than he loved his nightly hunts behind the shops.

The big ginger tom lived in the factory manager's house, a palatial detached residence with a large garden where he basked on the swing seat in the sun.

He stretched amiably when anyone spoke to

him, minced indoors to eat cream and steamed plaice and, as a special weekly treat, a half-pound tin of red salmon, which he adored. He could eat by day and eat by night and still have room for more.

His mistress worshipped him and he flirted with her, fluttering his eyelids and squeezing his eyes to make them small. He would purr noisily with immense satisfaction as her slender red-nailed fingers stroked his snowy chest, brushed the richly striped ginger fur and caressed his nose. Sometimes, when he washed, he washed her also, and she was blissfully unaware that the tongue that licked her scented skin had been eating rat the night before.

Only the fox was lonely, deep in the dusty ground, without a mate to run with, or a son to follow him, and with every man against him.

He slept, and waited for the drums to rouse him to excitement again. Most summers, when the sun was warm, he basked among the heather, enjoying the heat, but this year he had to hide. In his deep den, the earth was powdered and dusty and the air around him was so hot that at times he gasped for breath.

The fox was tempted by the scent of water from the sheep troughs on the farm.

But he did not dare to try and drink.

The guncrack was too terrifying to risk.

5 The Old Huntsman

The farmer glimpsed the fox several times in the next few weeks, as the animal returned from the town, skirting the farm cautiously. The man was up earlier, day by day, fighting the heavy buckets to take water to the beasts. They came listlessly to drink, and anger flared each morning as he saw their sorry condition.

There was little milk from the cattle.

The growing wool on the sheep was stained with dingy red dust.

Every farm suffered.

That was no consolation to a man nearing exhaustion. His wife helped him, filling the endless buckets for him to carry, the sound of running water for ever in her ears, by day and night.

Often she came to the door of the house and stared out over the fields where the hot sun shim-

43

mered, making mirages of water in the dancing air. If only it would rain. . . .

The farmer spoke to the Huntsman again, and he promised he would go hunting, just as soon as the autumn winds crisped the leaves and the sun lost its wicked strength. It was not soon enough. The fox must be dead by then, the farmer thought, and he made a trap.

He made it of wood and steel. He made it strong. He made it fierce. The steel jaws were governed by a spring that almost tore the farmer's finger from his hand when it snapped back, before he had set it firm. The finger was a throbbing reminder, day and night, of the reason for the injury.

The fox must die.

The fox must die before he came to feast on the starving sheep, to take the geese and ducks and hens, to steal the few surviving sources of money.

The Hunstman was very old. He saddled his nag daily, and daily removed the saddle, without ever mounting the horse; putting it now in the bathroom and now across his bed, now on the floor of the barn, now across the trunk of the old oak that the wind had torn from the ground and that bent gnarled branches towards the sky. Sometimes he remembered where he had put it and sometimes he did not, having to hunt through the cottage and barn and stable, using his horn to help him remember what he was seeking. The mellow notes excited the hounds, and the sound of their baying alerted the farmer, who stared wearily across the fields, wondering at the old fool and his calls to hunt nothing. He did not know the old man was searching for his saddle, but unable to find it because his brain was filled with memories of long ago hunts that he lived over and over again.

The day they found at Valley Bottom, and chased the fox over Hangman's Edge, running down the scree towards Longfisher Bridge, along the high road, between the cottages, where the villagers came to watch the loping red rover, the yelling hounds spilling behind it, deafened by thunder of the horses, the shouts and bellows of the men, by the call of the horn and the excited shrieks of children pounding the line the beast had taken.

The Huntsman was a young man again, his aches and pains forgotten. His knobbled rheumaticky hands were firm and slim and brown, holding lightly onto the reins. Was he riding Sarymay, the little grey mare with the gentle ways, or Darkfiend, the black devil that soared the fences as if he were possessed, or was it little dainty Dewdrop, who loved to steal bread from the baker's van and ice cream from the children, stretching out her long neck and nibbling it daintily from the cone?

The Huntsman lifted his horn.

It sang the Gone to Earth.

The fox had run from Devil's Dyke to Weird Man's Ditch, from the Century Field to the Rabble River, along the bank and over the hill into Nine Acre Patch and out again at Swineman's Cottage, and over again to the Listening Tree and onto the moor.

That had been a hunt to remember.

The Huntsman sounded the Gone to Earth again, and picked up the saddle from the kitchen table. He carried it outside, and thought to saddle the mare and ride, but the sun was too hot. He took the saddle into the kitchen, but the sun baked through the door and the leather would crack and spoil.

He carried it outside again, Hellhound following at his heels, while Beldame and Harridan slept, stretched out in the shade at the side of the house, and Dimdog, always stupid, sat in the sun, panting. His mother had been a hound who had wandered. The Huntsman had no idea who his father had been, but had kept the pup, curious to know how much hunting instinct it had inherited. The father must have been stupid, the Huntsman often thought. Dimdog looked vaguely like a hound, till you saw his hocks and his plumed tail and too sharp muzzle, the pointed ear that sometimes stuck straight up on end, giving him an appearance that was slightly lunatic. He had never learned sense.

The Huntsman put the saddle down and led Dimdog into the shade. He licked the man's hand, and promptly returned to the sunbaked step.

The Huntsman gave up and took his saddle into the barn. It was very cool here, though the straw and dust stood on the air, thick and throat choking. It was cooler than the house. The Hunstman scooped a pail of water from the standing barrel and put it for the dogs. Hellhound drank. Dimdog was too hot to move. The other two slept on.

There was something he had to do—
He had to chase a fox.

A fox that had stolen the farmer's hens.

The Huntsman scratched his head.

The sun would spoil the saddle. It was cooler here than indoors. He put the saddle on the floor and carefully covered it with hay. It would be safe there, and the leather would not crack. He sprinkled the hay with water.

He had not eaten that morning.

He went indoors to find an egg and cook it. But he had put the eggs in the bread bin the day before, lest Dimdog stole them. Dimdog had a liking for eggs, and would carry one around for hours, before crunching it slowly and feeling the delectable liquid trickle slimily down his throat.

The Huntsman could not remember where he had put the eggs.

Potatoes would do instead.

He peeled a potato, put it on the table and went outside. Slowly, the potato went browner and browner, and when the Huntsman came in again he looked at it in astonishment, wondering what it was doing there, and threw it away.

Hellhound took it and chewed it and spat it out.

He barked, and the Huntsman remembered he had not fed the dogs. Now he concentrated, opening tins, mixing meal and filling the bowls with water. Once he had fed a whole kennel full of dogs, fed them on raw meat bought when the farmers had stillborn animals. Now the hounds had not teeth for meat and neither had he. He scooped a little meat from the tin and licked his finger.

He was very hungry.

He fed the beasts and went indoors to find some bread.

The eggs were in the bread bin.

He boiled three eggs, and took them into the barn to eat them, using his fingers, as he could not find a spoon or knife and fork. He tidied the kitchen the day before and decided to keep the cutlery in his sideboard. He had completely forgotten. The empty drawer bewildered him and he shook his head.

When he had eaten the eggs he lay in the straw and slept. Hellhound ate the shells and then slept too, head across the old man's shoes. Dimdog wandered to the empty bed of the stream and looked at it thoughtfully. He found the tepid water in the bowl and drank, and sighed deeply. This time he crept into the shade and dreamed twitching dreams of the days when he was young and led the hunt and followed the fox.

The sun crept over the horizon.

Twilight brushed the moor.

The bats twittered and woke, stretching leathery wings. They skittered through the air, sweeping out of the barn in a cloud and harried the insects that blackened the sky. The hounds fled for shelter away from the sting and the suck of midges and gnats, and the Huntsman woke, puzzled to find himself in the barn and not in his rocking-chair in the kitchen.

The sun had vanished, and the night was a glittering mass of brilliant stars.

Far away over the moors the factory flare-off banished the dark for a brief moment, and then the night was blacker than before. The Huntsman had something to do.

He had to hunt a fox.

He went to find his saddle, but it had vanished, and it was almost morning before he gave up the search and retired to sleep, a brittle, half wakeful, old man's doze, in which he hunted again over trails and galloped up the screes, and mastered his horse.

He dreamed he was swimming in a river.

He dreamed of water, water falling from the sky, water pouring over the rocks, water, cool and sweet, banishing the dust. The panting hounds slept in his room. Dimdog, dreaming too, whimpered and thumped a leg.

The Huntsman woke to brilliant day and a merciless sun.

He ached with thirst.

He had something to do. He had to hunt a fox and to kill it for the farmer down the road.

He began to look for his saddle.

6   Johnny Toosmall

The endless days were a blaze of sunshine.

Never had Britain known such weather. Not even the Huntsman could recall such a summer.

The parched ground was baked hard.

Dust drifted on the air. Water ran tepid and rusty brown from the taps. The big rivers were so low between their banks that the fish died and the water stank. The tarns on the moors were only memories, their beds baked hard and cracked.

In the town the men called off the strike and emptied the foetid bins. It did little good. The bins filled again. The food in them rotted. The rats returned nightly.

The two policemen in the prowl car shuddered as the repulsive bodies were caught in the head-lamps' gleam. The fox saw one large grey veteran die beneath the giant-eyed monster that rumbled swiftly through the streets, its shadow out-pacing its spinning wheels. So the monster also killed. The fox hid after that when he heard its angry voice mutter as the car climbed the slope, the high-pitched note changing to a scream as it crested the hill and the driver slipped out of fourth and into second gear, the cogs failing to mesh correctly. Its huge eyes lit up the street, sweeping round the corner as it fled.

The fox never saw the men inside. He had never seen a car by day. He only knew the dragon beast puffed black smoke from its bowels, and glared with enormous eyes, and trampled and crushed anything that lay in its path. The policemen tried deliberately to get rid of the teeming rats, knowing the plagues they brought. Sickness, and sometimes death. Their bites were loaded with poison, so that the wounds festered and healed slowly in puckered scars.

The wise rats knew the car brought death and hid too.

The nights were airless, so hot that people tossed and twisted and flung off their covers, longing for a cool breeze. Their sunburned bodies itched with bites from the plagues of midges and mosquitos. Babies whimpered in their cots, children cried and the women hushed them, and prayed for rain.

The farmer watched his fields sicken, the grain sour and crumble-dry, a hint only of what might have been. Little hot winds ran along the furrows and scoured the dust. Dust thickened in the farmhouse. Even the eggs on the nests were dusty in the morning, and the water from the tap did not wash them clean.

Eyes ached, and were grit-filled from dawn until dusk. At night the stars were so bright it hurt to look at them. The phantom horde left the wood and flooded over the moor, the mist behind it mysteriously pearled. The nights were filled with the ever louder beat of the drums, the call of the gathering army, that seemed to grow in volume with the increasing heat of the year. The farmer and his wife lay awake, hearts thudding in time to the muffled thump of the pounding sticks.

At dawn the sounds faded.

The farmer rose from his sleepless bed, put on his coat and jeans and went to the barn where he worked on his trap. His hand was still swollen and throbbed and his wife dressed it morning and night, but it would not heal. It reminded him, minute by minute, of his enemy the fox. He pictured the fox waiting for the sheep to die; he pictured the fox lying beyond the wall, watching the weakening geese and ducks, waiting to steal the bodies that would fetch a pound or so in the town.

The farmer fought the trap, beating into it all his hatred, making it strong and firm and true so that it would catch the fox and break his back, and free the beasts from danger.

The farmer's wife grew thinner. Her hands were raw from lifting the endless buckets. The farmer dreamed of carrying buckets, of buckets with holes in them so that the water ran out and soaked uselessly into the ground; of empty buckets, because the tap had run dry. The sun danced in front of his eyes, a giant red globe that etched itself on his eyeballs so that when he came indoors he saw a multitude of suns hanging in the dusty air, masking the furniture and the wallpaper.

The farmer's wife spent her evenings praying

for rain. Her husband did not share her religion. He watched her leave when the work was ended and the sun went down, watched her walk across the empty moors to the little church at the edge of the town.

Inside was peace when she knelt at the foot of the serene Madonna, who held her babe close against her skyblue robes, a smile on her gentle lips. Once the farmer's wife had prayed to Mary to send her a son, but now she was glad her prayers had never been answered. There was little enough for herself and her man, and she could not have borne to watch a child of hers suffer as they were suffering.

Then the farmer's wife knelt at the foot of the cross where Jesus hung for ever, his body contorted in the agony of death. He had known pain, he had known the need to endure, to triumph over misfortune; he had known tragedy. He had known pity.

She needed so much to pray.

Where were the words?

A memory teased her mind, drifted through the haze of exhaustion, a memory of herself in a long white nightdress, kneeling by her childhood bed.

Gentle Jesus, meek and mild,
Look upon this little child.
Pity my simplicity
Suffer me to come to thee.

She toiled home in the dusk. Bats were flaunting on the searing breeze, swift black shadows, darker than twilight.

Beyond her, in the wood, the drum beats echoed faintly.

Behind them came the sound of hammering as

her husband worked at the trap.

The fox watched her, hidden. He was waiting for the yellow patchworked windows to darken, so that he could make his way to the town and join the cats in their nightly war.

The Huntsman saw the farmer's wife as she passed. He had just fallen over his saddle, having gone into the barn to find a straying hen and see if she had laid in the straw. He could not understand what the saddle was doing there. Dimdog followed him, close against his knee, loving the Huntsman even more than he loved food, never wanting to let the old man out of his sight.

The Huntsman pushed him away fretfully, preferring Harridan for all her wicked flighty ways, and her obvious adoration of him only for the food he gave her. Dimdog came for caresses in the morning. Harridan waited at the pantry door, her mind in her stomach and nowhere else. Her tail only wagged when she was given food. Dimdog wagged his tail whenever he saw his master, overcome with a joy too great to express, so that his whole body was an ecstacy of greeting.

The Huntsman nodded to the farmer's wife.

She tried to smile, failed, nodded in her turn and hurried on.

The drumbeats followed her. She ran, reaching the farmhouse door just at the pipes' wild skirl sounded above the drums. She slammed the door and hastily lit the lamp which the farmer had forgotten. Shadows flickered and danced in the dusty room, and fear danced with them.

The fox was a rumour of movement, a swift slide along the ground, a tongue drinking. The exhausted sheep were too weary to bleat, too tired to run. The fox finished his drink and was gone, padding across ground still hot from the day's penance. He padded at the edges of the fields, padded along the alleyway, avoided the chemicals on the grass and shuddered to a halt behind a garden wall just as the dragon-eyed monster swept along the road, growling savagely. Its voice flared to an ear-splitting bellow as the driver sounded the horn to alert Bludgeon and Brainstorm who were running side by side down the centre of the road, used to cars by day as well as night, and unafraid. They sped to the side of the road and watched, their eyes glinting in the headlights.

'Need more of those,' the driver said, referring to the cats, shuddering as he saw a rat flash under the fence and vanish. He loathed the town at night.

The car windows were open, but the foetid stench of the rotting bins and the stink of chemicals was often so overpowering that it was better to swelter. The mens' jackets lay on the back seat. Their rolled shirtsleeves revealed sunburnt arms, and buttons were undone to free dark brown throats.

The two policemen were glad they worked during the night. The days were merciless; the sun reflected a million times, blinding from other cars, from windscreen and mirror and shop window. They slept by day, in airless rooms where curtains shielded the worst of the light, and they had no need of any covers.

They stopped at the factory gate to check with the night watchman.

There was a new man, a tiny man, barely five feet tall. He had begun work a few weeks ago. He loved his job. Before this he had worked by day with men who towered above him, who frightened him by their strength and teasing, but now, here, alone, the world was his own and he was king. He had endured the teasing men for fifteen miserable years, and had gladly changed when offered the chance, as no one else would stay. He always did his work well—and now he had his own domain.

He was lord of the great machines that throbbed and hissed and thumped and thundered. He was lord of the cats that came to him for milk.

He learned their names: Buster and Bouncer, Bludgeon and Brainstorm and Bobby One-eye. He loved cats beyond all other animals. Here he was able to sit and watch them for hours as they stretched and prowled, and moved slinkily between the furniture, or pounced and patted, lean elegant bodies more beautiful than anything else in the world. Perhaps he loved them most because they were all that he was not; grace and charm, and power to kill their enemies without blame or punishment. Also, they were smaller than he.

He had to watch the machinery, walk between the towering chimneys, and look at the dials. He was responsible for seeing that the green light in his office was always on and never replaced by the terrifying red signal that meant he must sound the alarm, alert the fire brigade and call in the heavy squad to avert danger. It would mean danger more terrifying than fire over the moors, for here fire would bring explosion upon explosion and destroy the town.

Their safety depended on him.

By night, he was the most important man in the place; perhaps one of the most important in the world, for if this factory stopped then a great many others would suffer in every country under the sun, as it manufactured a valuable raw material. He had never felt important before.

Nor was he afraid of the army that marched among the chimneys. He could see them plainly. They were shadows, doing no harm. They had no tongues to torment him, calling him Tiny and Tich and Johnny Toosmall. He owned the nighttime world, the brilliant moon, the glittering stars, the black-and-white cats and the great machines.

He made tea for the two policemen, who were both kind and did not make him feel insignificant. They listened to him when he talked. All the time he watched the telltale, lest it spring into life and he had to sound the alarm.

When the men had gone he thought he saw a shadow move from the gate. He heard the sound of lapping. He narrowed his eyes, able to see almost as well in the dark as the cats.

It was the fox. He felt pity for the beast, dusty coated, slit eared, mangy furred, an outcast like himself. He did not move.

The animal slipped away.

Next night, remembering, the fox returned and found a bowl of milk waiting for him and, beside it, a plate full of tinned dog meat, which he ate voraciously.

This was better than eating rats, although it was never enough to fill him. It gave him strength to hunt.

Soon he called at the factory every night. The watchman hid in the shadows and waited, delighting in the knowledge that he was enabling the wild creature to stay alive.

57

He knew the fox would help the cats with the ratting.

Once, long ago, Johnny Toosmall had lived in the country.

The fox reminded him of the sound of bees in the heather and the wind on the shadowy hill, when he ran free, a barefoot child, knowing nothing of the difficulties of being grown up. All his friends were small then.

He, the cats and the fox owned the night, the moon and the stars.

He whistled softly as he watched the moving dials and noted the time at every hour, and wrote, in a neat hand in beautiful copperplate, that the light was green.

He whistled the song that the drums sang as the army moved out each evening, but he did not even know that he echoed the tune.

The fox heard the whistling and learned that he could trust one man.

7   Drought

Day succeeded pitiless day.

Water was rationed in the towns and the villages. Out on the moors, even on the mountains, many of the springs and wells ran dry for the first time in living memory. Only those streams that hid deep down in the earth poured into the daylight, spilled on the rocks, and were sucked dry by the searing sun.

The reservoirs from which the water came were dusty pools between mud-baked banks. The rivers were low between the banks and were so polluted that all water had to be boiled. No one dared drink it straight from the pipes. Illness that men had forgotten came to plague the people. The nights were noisy with the crying of fretful children.

The churches were crowded with men and women praying for rain.

Rain to fill the rivers and the lakes and the pools

59

and the tarns. Rain to fatten the drying grain; rain to swell the shrivelled peas; to ripen the fruit that hung on the trees, or that dropped and fell, covered in hordes of tiny black insects, to rot on the ground, where it was pecked up by starving birds.

It was necessary to disinfect the streets. The rank choking smell of strong disinfectant lay everywhere.

The farmer and his wife had water in their taps two hours every morning and two hours every evening. They worked to fill the troughs, carrying the endless buckets, passing one another without a word, too weary to think. They stumbled as they walked, almost sleepwalking.

The Huntsman also had water at dawn and dusk. He filled his buckets and his pans and his washbasin. Then he took his saddle and polished it until the leather gleamed and reflected the sun; he polished his high boots until he could see his face reflected in them; he burnished the silver top of the whip that had been given him by the Master of the Hunt when he retired, a beautiful chased silver foxhead, a gift to treasure. He burnished his horn.

He was an old man and he had not much time left. Soon, he knew, he would close his eyes and never waken again, and when he did so he wished to be found with all his possessions in the condition in which he had kept them as a young man. He sat and rocked and polished all night. It was far too hot to sleep. He welcomed the drums. He tapped his foot to the quick gay music.

He was sad at dawn when the retreat sounded and the weeping women passed him, their faces clearer now. Perhaps his great-great grandmother was among them. Perhaps he would join the horde that travelled the moor at night. He wondered, unafraid. He had lived a long life, done harm to no one except perhaps a few foxes. Death would come kindly—a long sleeping after a lifetime of working. He beat softly on the saddle, his gnarled fingers keeping time with the knell of the nightly drums.

The farmer could think of nothing but the fox. He knew it was the cause of all his troubles. It was a devil, a witch thing, that had brought disaster to him. It was the cause of the remorseless sun; it was the cause of his starving beasts; it was the cause of all his misery. If only he could kill it, all would be well. The sky would cloud again, rain would fall again and his farm would be saved.

The farmer's wife knew that the wicked weather was to punish men for their arrogance; for their evil ways; for their denial of God. Men fought, they stole, they lied, they cheated, they mocked. They filled the earth with their ugly cities, they tore down the wild places, they worshipped the television set and the motor car. Until men changed, there could be no release for any of them. She prayed, night after night, begging, not for rain, but for a change of heart in man, for pity and compassion, for a return to simplicity.

It was so hot in the town that Johnny Toosmall dared not take his eyes from the green telltale. He was afraid the heat would evaporate the water in the huge cooling towers; and then the temperature would rise and the town would be lost, for nothing could save them. The tanks would explode.

He was more afraid of that than of the nightly army. He watched the telltale and watched the ghostly skirmishes and wondered if ghosts had feelings and if they saw him. He wondered if they knew that this bit of moor on which they had fought had gone and been replaced by towering steel chimneys and giant tanks, by steam pipes and condensers, by huts and brick offices and laboratories.

Or did they still see the barren moor and the bushes and trees which had given them brief shelter and false security, more than a hundred years ago? Did they see him, Johnny Toosmall, walking his territory, checking his machinery, calling his cats? Did they see the cats as they slipped homewards in the dawn? Did they see the fox? Were they there? Were they real, visible to all, or was he creating them, inventing them out of his loneliness and his need to people the dark, not with real men who would mock and tease him, but with phantoms that he could pity for their lives were sadder than his. Or was it he who was the ghost, he and the factory, while they were reality?

There was so much time to think at night, when only he, the cats, the rats, the fox and the two policemen were awake and walking about their business.

There was time to look at the stars and to know that they dwarfed all men, not only him; and then he strutted with the pride of a cock robin and his bright robin eyes laughed up at the moon.

Each hour he wrote in the book in his beautiful

neat copperplate. Wrote that the factory was checked, that every machine was working perfectly, that the green safe light showed that all was well in his domain.

He brought milk for the cats. The milk was thin, without cream, and tasted odd so he boiled it, wondering if the cattle were diseased. The cats came, one by one, slipping silently through the door. Bouncer stepped lightly and Bludgeon walked slowly. Buster was always gay and greeted Johnny, weaving round his legs, mewing affectionately, arching to the hand that stroked him. Brainstorm was dainty, light footed, and raced in, an excited slip of a cat, leaping to Johnny Toosmall's shoulder, to rub against his neck and purr. Lastly came Bobby One-eye, wary, distrustful, sidling round the wall until he came to his own saucer, placed away from the other cats. Only when he had fed would he relax and jump to Johnny's knee. If the policemen came for their tea after Bobby had come home, they found only four cats, for Bobby was hidden behind the tool box that stood in the corner.

Lastly, when all was quiet, came the fox.

Johnny waited for him, hidden in the shadows. The fox was a loner, like himself, friendless, alien, unwanted. Perhaps one day Johnny would master the beast's distrust. Perhaps the fox would allow him to stroke him, as he stroked the cats; would feed from his hands. Johnny's heart thumped with excitement at the thought. To master a wild thing. That was something that few men could do. It was an ambition to cherish.

The food smelled of Johnny's hands.

The milk bowl smelled of Johnny's hands.

The fox could smell Johnny himself in the darkness. He ate and drank, unafraid. The smell of Johnny was the smell of the milk that saved his life, for the water was too foul to drink, except on the farm, where he rarely dared to go. Only when thirst overmastered him did he risk the sounding gun.

The fox slipped out of the factory, following the retreating shades hidden in the mist that surrounded them.

Johnny waited for day to come, and then clocked off and went home to the little garret at the other end of the town where he sweltered under the roof and longed for the night.

8   The Trap

The farmer knew that the rain would come only when the fox was dead.

He had finished the trap. There never had been such a trap. The base was of gleaming wood, polished until it shone, made strong and thick and true, a heavy base to hold the wicked steel. The steel spring was so strong that the razor edge would kill the fox at once as it snapped back.

The farmer's wife said nothing.

Her husband was crazy. The fox had nothing to do with the weather and though she believed in the devil, she did not believe in witchcraft.

That day the farmer left the watering to his wife. He hunted the moors, searching for the run most used by the fox. He found a mountain ash tree, a few leaves left on the brittle twigs, a few green berries clinging to the harsh barked branches. The bark was brittle and flaking.

Witches hated the rowan.

The farmer picked the largest twig and lashed it to the trap with twine. That would settle the fox.

He found the den, deep in the roots of the tree.

There was a run between the clumps of bracken. There were telltale feathers here, from the bodies of dead birds that the fox had found on the moor.

The farmer set the trap.

He pulled the bracken and covered it.

The fox was curled in his den. He could smell the farmer and knew the man was there. He crouched, silent, holding his breath. The dusty air outside the den vibrated in the shimmering heat. The farmer wiped his gritty hands across his sweating face.

He tramped away, the noise of his booted feet alerting every beast within miles. The ground vibrated as he trod.

'It will rain tonight,' the farmer said.

His wife looked at him.

She looked at the dazzling sky.

She looked at the mountains. There was not a cloud anywhere. Only the heat that mocked her, that made the air dance, that shimmered above the pan of water boiling on the gas. The kitchen sweltered.

Her husband was a fool.

Day ended at last. The distant mountains were black. The town glowed on the southern horizon. The flare-off from the chimneys flashed red and was gone. The moors stretched darkly.

The drums began.

The fox left his earth.

He paused at the opening and sniffed the air. His nose was hot and dry and he licked it to moisten it. It was easier to scent with a damp nose.

Smell of the farmer, rank on the ground.

Smell of the farmer, sharp on the air.

Smell of the farmer, foul on the bracken.

He moved, step by slow step, questioning the night-time breeze. He was drowned in the farmer's smell. He tensed his muscles. His slit ear pricked, listening.

Sound of the drums, familiar and unfrightening.

The dry whisper of a grasshopper, a faint persistent chirring.

The *whoop whoop whoop* of the hunting owl, bound for the town and for carnage among the rat-ridden bins.

The soft sigh of the wind, trickling in the grass.

A squeak and then silence, as the hidden mouse smelled fox above the mansmell.

The fox stood still, summoning memory. The man had gone; there was no sound of him; no sound of heavy breathing, of footsteps on the ground; yet his smell lay everywhere. He must have left something of himself behind.

The fox could not reason, but he could recognize danger.

Instincts sharper than the razor edge of the trap warned him.

He stepped along the path, one slow paw succeeding another. His pads had healed, but were not yet hard again and he could feel the gritty soil beneath them, could feel the discomfort of a sharp-edged stone pricking at him, could feel the prick of thistle and the dry crumble of dead leaves.

The shape of the path was wrong.

Where there had been a clear run the night

before there was now a hump, a mound of pulled bracken and a smell of dead rabbit, all overlaid with mansmell. And another smell.

The smell of oil on metal.

He had smelled that smell before, long ago, as a cub. He had watched a poacher set a snare; had seen the old badger come from his earth, snarling to his mate and his cubs to stay still, not to move a paw or a whisker, while he was busy.

The fox sniffed at the bracken.

He knew what would happen if he tugged at the rabbit.

He pulled the bracken away with his teeth, careful to work gently, teasing at every stem until the trap was free, a wicked shimmer in the moonlight, the rabbit, tempting and mouth watering, stretched innocently along the wood, begging to be eaten.

The trap would remain an ever present danger.

The fox leaped in the air and somersaulted, smiting the metal with his furred spine. The movement triggered the spring. The steel teeth slammed shut. The fox leaped free. He had sprung the trap from behind, had rendered the lethal jaws harmless. He pulled at the rabbit, but it smelled of man and a new sense warned him. He left the trap and loped to the town, and warred with the rats, hunting them for the pleasure of hunting and not for food.

Johnny Toosmall waited in the shadows, and watched the fox slip quietly through the little gate, run over the ground, and come warily to the tiny patch besides the watchman's hut. There was no danger of chemicals here.

The fox fed daintily; he licked his chops, and washed his face with a slender paw.

The police car drew up outside.

The fox was gone, mingling with the fighting shadows that waged constant war behind the first cooling tower. He knew which paths to follow; knew, now, the scent of the chemical that had burned his paws and avoided it, running swiftly past the tubs of brown sun-crisped plants, past the managing director's office window, along the front drive, into the street to the edge of the town, following the straggle across the moor to curl and sleep again as the drumbeats faded, and the day woke to the sultry shine of the unrelenting sun.

The farmer returned to his trap and stared in disbelief.

It was sprung, but no fox lay dead between its ferocious jaws. Only the torn body of the rabbit and there, on the grass all round it, the bodies of three dead crows that had pecked at the poisoned carcase.

They must have triggered the spring.

He set the trap again.

That night the fox rolled again: the spring flashed and the jaws crashed together again and the fox ran off.

It became a duel, with the fox winning.

At last the farmer knew the truth.

This was no live beast but a ghost fox, a devil indeed, a vision to torment him, belonging with the other visions that roamed the moor.

That night, he went with his wife to church.

9 The Phantom Army

Most people heard nothing and saw nothing of the fleeting shades, as they walked on the moors, or walked near the factory late at night, or walked along the road that bordered the graveyard. But they knew fear—fear of the clinging mist that hid the sharpness of nearby objects, fear of the racked trees where the wind moaned with a shivery sound, like the sobbing of women and children, fear of desolation.

The Huntsman saw.

The Huntsman heard.

So did the farmer's wife, so did Johnny Too-small and so did the children.

The farmer heard but did not see.

There was not enough water to fill the buckets for the mare. Daily the Huntsman carried her meagre ration to her. Daily he wilted himself, becoming smaller and greyer, a dried up shadow of

a man, grieving as he watched the horse he loved grow thinner, and knew she was near to death. She was so very old.

She could not eat. Her dry throat could not make enough saliva to swallow the strawlike grass. She drank greedily, but there was never enough. The Huntsman spent the long day moving her from one patch of shade to the next, but he knew her steps faltered and her head hung low. He ached with sorrow.

He kept his saddle on the kitchen table now, with the curtains drawn to guard it from the sun. He had to polish it, again and again to keep it free from dust. He polished the fox-headed silver crop; he rubbed the reins and the bridle and shone the metal; and he took a fox's brush, mounted on a wooden base, from the cupboard under the stairs and put it on the dresser. It was an ancient brush, the fur coppery and brittle, long forgotten till now.

Memory eased the scorching days.

The Huntsman brought the hounds into the kitchen out of the sun, and even Dimdog came gratefully. The old man rocked in his chair and the wooden rockers creaked as he swayed. The patchwork cushion had been gay once, but now was dingy behind his head. As he swayed he hummed to himself softly and tried not to think of his dying mare.

The cottage was stifling at night. The Huntsman could never stay indoors. He pushed and dragged the rocking-chair across the kitchen and sat on the porch. But even the wind was hot, a wicked teasing wind that tossed the dust and sighed in the trees and was a constant background to the muffled drums. The hounds crept away from the drums. Each one sought sanctuary under a bed, or behind a bin in the barn, or behind a cupboard in the house.

Once the army had been shadowy; moving wraiths, keeping time to the lilting songs. Now they marched purposefully and the Huntsman thought they had changed their path, leaving the moor behind, approaching the road that led past his house and on to the brooding factory that lowered at the edge of the moor.

He could see the army more plainly each night. The drummer, an eager stocky man, his kilt swinging, his plaid fastened by a circular brooch, the light shining on the handle of the dirk that he wore in his sock. The shadows flickered across the twirling sticks, and patterned mens' bearded faces, and the faces of the women, far behind them, moving slowly, heads down and babes in their arms and children clinging to their skirts.

Drrrum, Drummmm . . . Drrrumm.

A quick rhythm, a stirring beat, a moment of triumph, as the army became more visible, marching towards him, man after man turning his head to look long at the old man sitting and rocking. Eyes glinted, mouths smiled, a hand lifted.

They were hidden and misty, and then they were gone, and the Huntsman was aware of a great longing within him, of an envy of the horde that roamed at night, of a tiredness that engulfed him, so that his body ached and longed for rest. Not the brief rest of the passing night, but the benison of knowing that his time was ended, and that all he had done had been well done.

He waited and watched and when dawn was a

74

whisper of distant light he saw the defeated rabble horde flying to the shelter of the woods.

The woods.

These were not the barren leafless woods of his latter years, but for a moment the trees reared tall against the sky, in full leaf. The wind bowed the branches and the tall trunks tried to touch the ground. There were men among them, running men, dying men, bleeding men. Men who helped one another; men who turned on one another, and among them went the women, with a sorrowing noise such as the Huntsman had never heard before.

He struck his hands together, sure that his heart would break.

Dawn flared over the horizon.

The red sun leaped in the sky.

The wind died.

The Huntsman eased his aching body out of the chair. His legs were so stiff he could scarcely walk. His hands were cramped. His eyes ached with watching.

He looked towards the woods. Sparse and spare and stunted, the trees groped towards the sky, forced into alien shapes by the endless wind.

The Huntsman took the bucket and turned on the tap.

There was a trickle of water in the bucket; there was a little water in the kettle. He added the two together and walked wearily across the yard. He narrowed his eyes at the glare of the sun.

He could not see the mare.

She should have been standing at the entrance to the barn, waiting for him. He walked into the shadows.

She lay there, dead. The years had at last defeated her.

He sat beside her stroking her soft muzzle, remembering.

She had been young and strong and beautiful and a major part of his past, carrying him effortlessly all day, as he chased the foxes that killed the ducks and hens and the geese. One had even killed a swan one year. He had forgotten that swan.

He wanted to walk again in a green meadow that he knew where the flowers grew tall, and a shallow brook babbled over the rocky bed. He yearned to paddle in it. He wanted to swim round the curve of the bank and see the deep clear pool and the two swans floating in endless leisure.

Cool clear water.

Cool deep water.

His mare was dead.

He was an old man again, sitting in the dust. His eyes and his throat ached. He smoothed the curve of her neck and left her. He could not bury her alone. Perhaps the farmer would come later in the day.

That night the drums were loud and clear, resounding as the men marched. The men were larger, towering above the moor. Their feet thumped on the ground. The drummer led them, his moving hands flickering.

The drummer was close enough to see in every detail; the neat beard on his face, the curl in his hair, the laughter in his eyes.

He reached out his hand. The drumstick touched the Huntsman on the shoulder.

The army faded and was gone.

The world had ended for the Huntsman. Dimdog knew it and came and sniffed, and broke his heart, and joined his master. The other hounds sat in a row and howled.

The farmer and his wife heard the howling and knew what it meant. They walked across the moor.

Four days later a small funeral procession moved towards the churchyard. The vet had put the hounds to sleep. They were old, too.

The farmer's wife prayed in church for the Huntsman's soul.

She had thought, that night, that the moving armies were real. She had seen them more clearly than ever before, but now she knew she was mistaken.

There were only shapes in the writhing mists, and over all the cachinnation of the drums.

The farmer grieved because the Huntsman now would never hunt the fox.

There would be no rain until the fox was dead.

The farmer was obsessed.

He returned to the farm to build another snare, a stronger snare, a more cunning snare, a snare that would end his problems for ever.

His wife watched him and listened.

She heard the pipes and she heard the drums.

She thought she heard the thunder of hooves and the sweet faint call of the hunting horn sounding the View-Halloo, and then the baying of a pack of hounds, nosedown on a trail with only one ending.

She watched the sun rise and set and prayed for rain. She watched the cattle she had tended so long.

Lord have mercy on us.

Mary, Mother of Heaven, have pity upon us and send us rain.

10   Danger!

Nothing had changed.

The moor was more desolate now. The Huntsman's cottage was empty. The door hung open and swung wide. Rats and mice ate the food that was left, and vanished again. There were no more crumbs.

A swallow roosted in the kitchen dresser.

Birds came in for shade.

Nothing stirred in the empty rooms. The dust swirled and thickened on the abandoned furniture. The cushions on the rocking-chair were dingy grey, the bright pattern long ago forgotten.

At night the marching army closed around the cottage. Sometimes a hunting horn, sweet and clear, echoed softly behind the marching drums. The chair rocked, but there was no one there.

The fox heard the horn.

He heard the drums; he curled more tightly,

trying to keep the dust from his aching eyes. He would never be clean again. The damaged pads had healed, but were hard and scaly; they irritated when he walked. He no longer ran. He moved slowly, fighting the heat, his mouth open, panting. Dust covered his tongue.

Even the water in the taps was brackish now. The farmer had no time for his new snare. He had only time to fill the buckets and drag them to the fields; to stop and wipe his arm across his sweating face, and drink a few drops of tepid water.

The sky was cloudless still.

Clear and blue, with a blazing sun.

The fox earth crumbled and the ground caved in. The fox tried to dig, but the soil was baked so brittle that no tunnel would hold. He curled in the tree roots that held him secure, but the sun walked endlessly across the sky and the shadows shifted and the heat scorched his skin.

That night dusk was accompanied by flickering lightning that flashed on the hills; that blazed on the moor, leaving darkness ever deeper behind it; that struck a far away tree, riving it in two with the crash of doom.

The fox ran.

This was a noise greater than any gun he had ever heard. Not only the farmer threw death with a stick; the skies raged too, and out of them came an enormous terror inspiring drumbeat that drowned the marching phantoms, that echoed the beating drums, that throbbed on the shimmering air.

Johnny Toosmall looked at his dials and was afraid.

If one zigzag flashed on his highest tower, the world would end for the town that night.

He prayed as he walked; an anxious little man, conscious that the safety of the people beyond the gates depended on him alone. He could not rest. He wandered from tower to steam turbines, from generators to offices, wandered over the dead grass and again and again went back to the master light, to the big green monitor that told him all was well.

He was aware of power.

Of power that heated the steam, that ran along the cables, that stirred the great vats. Power that surged and seethed and pulsed. The steam pipes echoed the drums. The thunder rolled in the sky. The lightning cracked and flared.

If only it would rain.

Johnny Toosmall returned to the little hut that housed his desk and a chair and a kettle that would boil water for his tea. He could not drink tea tonight. He was so hot that sweat darkened his soaking shirt; so hot that his trousers clung to his pricking body; so hot that his hair was wet against his head; so hot that trickles marked his face, and he tried to dry them with a towel that had long ago become a soaked and dirty rag.

The prowl car patrolled the streets.

The car windows were all wide open.

The men were stripped to their shirt sleeves, but that did not bring comfort. Their throats were dry and ached with the dust that choked them. Dust surrounded the car, almost masking it so that Bobby One-eye, leaping the wall, saw a devil cloud sweep down the street with a glow behind it and fled to Johnny Toosmall for comfort.

A fireball hung on the air, far away over the moor. The police car stopped and the men stared as the glow drifted and expanded and then hit the ground with such a crack that the people thought the factory had exploded at last. Every light went on in the town.

The police car speeded down the road, blue light flashing. It roared through the factory gates, the dust flying high behind it.

Johnny Toosmall met them, white-faced.

They raced to look at the monitor.

The telltale glowed green—green and cool—the deep colour of the restless sea, the clear colour of a grassy glade, the pure colour of an unflawed emerald.

The three men stared at one another and relaxed.

Beyond the towers the sky was coloured again and again, as sheets of lightning streamed across the night; yellow, blue, green, violet, rose, flaming on the horizon, blinding human eyes.

The fox ran, and crouched and hid his eyes under his paws. He was afraid, almost to death. He shivered at each frightening glimpse of an alien world, each tree stark, each house black, each chimney outlined, and then the total light lack which defeated even his eyes.

He moved by scent alone when the world was hidden and the roll in the distance had died to a faint echo. Beyond and behind him came the drums.

The sound followed him all the way to the factory at the edge of the town, where he knew Johnny Toosmall would give him sanctuary.

11   The Telltale

Johnny Toosmall was afraid.

He was afraid with the fear of a soldier in battle; he was afraid with the fear of a policeman facing an armed man; he was afraid with the fear that haunts those who work with danger. The diver's fear of a broken air pipe; the steeplejack's fear of a ladder that gives way; the surging fear that comes to the men who dance with death in their work; miners in dark places, where firedamp and roof-fall menace unseen; firemen, fighting heat and smoke and flame and choking gas that might sweep beyond control; foresters, watching the tiny trickle of creeping smoke that spells disaster.

Johnny Toosmall was brave with the bravery of all these men. He fought his fear, and walked among the towers, and watched the flashes brighten the hills, watched the tongued lances drive towards his charges. He was the most responsible man in the town tonight. He stood proud and walked tall, and he returned again and again to the telltale.

It glowed clear and steady and green.

Each time he saw it he drew a swift sigh; each time he saw it he looked out at the night. He saw the prowl car drive away; he saw the fox limp towards him, defeated by fear.

He had very little water left. Enough in the kettle to last until morning. He had given more than half his ration to the cats. The panting fox was more in need than he.

He knelt and poured the last of his water into the bowl. The fox drank and crept out of the flickerflash night into the sanctuary of the little room. It lay for a while, panting. Johnny Toosmall looked at the clock.

Four in the morning and a long way to dawn.

He wrote in his immaculate copperplate in the big book that the foreman checked every morning.

4 a.m. Lightning all night. So far all well. The monitor is green.

The fox watched him, puzzled by the scratch of pen on paper. It lifted its head, ears pricked, and cocked its mask, first to one side and then to another.

Johnny Toosmall opened a tin of catfood and put it in the empty bowl. No more water for either of them tonight. No more tea but he did not care. The beast's eyes had lost some of their fear.

The fox did not move.

Johnny Toosmall knelt and put the bowl down close to the animal. The fox ate, too tired to rouse its body from the ground. It ate, head stretched

83

out, lying prone. Johnny Toosmall stroked the dusty skull.

The amber eyes looked up at him. The beast continued to feed.

Johnny Toosmall sat beside the fox. An enormous pride filled him. The wild animal had come to him for shelter. It had trusted him above all other men. He not only guarded the town. He had cast out fear in a creature of the woods, a beast that had never known man, except as an enemy.

The fox rested.

The man watched the sky blaze and fade; he listened to the growls in the hills and knew the storm was coming nearer.

He longed for the rain.

The air was still.

Hot and heavy, thickening the senses, making heads ache and bodies sweat. Deeply oppressive, the night was as great a torment as the sunbaked day.

The fox crept to the door.

The horizon flashed into blinding light.

Arcs of lightning sparked through the air.

The sky cracked open.

The deafening crash was above their heads, all around them, vibrating the ground and destroying the factory. Johnny Toosmall turned his head. The fox ran.

Out into the night, among the thrumming towers, beyond the hissing pipes towards the moor. Away from fear, away to leave the moor, to seek for shelter in a distant wood, where the soft horn never sounded, where the sky never broke into madness, where the days were cool and the nights were dark and there was peace to hunt.

Where there was water and food.

The fox ran, past the offices and past the sheds.

He did not fear the trickle that leaked from the crack in the big vat. He did not fear the poison plume that smoked on the air. He had seen mist so often on the moor.

The fumes caught him as he ran. He fell, twisting and choking, struggling for breath, gasping deep, only to suck more and more of the deadly gas into his lungs.

He died as the first drops of rain fell, slow and singly, on the concrete path.

Johnny Toosmall, passing that way a moment later on his patrol, saw the dead body and knew a great pity. He knelt, intending to carry the fox and bury it. The gas tore at his throat as a rushing wind swept it towards him.

He stood up and ran.

The white plume followed him, creeping along the ground, lifting into the air, seeping around corners, chasing after him.

It grabbed at his throat, it slowed his legs, it filled his head with visions.

He was running with an army.

The men were all around him, their eyes dancing, their drums beating, their pipes lilting. They moved with a swing and a swift skirl of kilts; they moved with pride; they swept around him and drove him forward with them so that his legs picked up the rhythm, his hands swung with them, and the world he knew was dim.

The factory was fading, a ghostly place that never was.

He had to warn the town.

He fought the phantoms, driving them out of his head.

They faded and he ran on, now fighting a weariness that overmastered him. He longed for sleep. He longed for clear air to breathe, for the storm to die away, for silence.

Thunder roared in his ears.

Then came the rain.

Rain, that fell out of clouds so low that the sky was blacker than the deepest pit. Only the fire-flakes flew from cloud to cloud blinding all eyes.

Johnny Toosmall could not breathe. He was soaked, his hair lay wet against his face, his clothes clung to his body, his heavy legs refused to obey him.

Walk, Johnny Toosmall. Walk.

Warn the town.

Check the telltale.

Press the alarm bell.

Sound the sirens so that they peal above the storm. People will die tonight, Johnny Toosmall. They'll die if you give up.

The voice was in his head.

It warred with his resisting body that longed to lie down and rest. Longed for clean clear air; longed to breathe deep, and ease lungs that were seared by the poisonous gas. It was all around him, lifting on the air in spite of the rain; thick and heavy, vaporous and cloying, choking, so that Johnny tore at his throat with agonized hands and forced his way on.

Drum, drum drum.

Ta tum, ta rum ta rum.

The drums beat. The pipes sounded. The hunting horn lilted.

The rain pelted down.

The rain would lay the gas.

The lightning had hit the big gas container; the crack was widening. The gas was swirling into the rain, misting across the ground, white and thick; a dense layer that deepened, while Johnny forced his way across the endless yard.

He was so small. Too small. The yard was lengthening as he ran. The hut was never nearer. The light was never brighter. The gas surrounded him, hiding the doorway.

The drummers about him were solid now; he could feel their shoulders rough against his shirt; he could, when his eyes cleared, see the jewelled brooches that held the plaids.

Light glinted from the lances. Light flared as the chimneys opened and let off smoke and flame.

Flame and gas and a flash of doom. If the gas leak grew . . . if the flare-off caught the gas. . . . Johnny ran. He ran and the army ran with him. He ran across the yard and arms held him and buoyed him and strengthened him; he ran and there were men helping him, lifting him, so that he was suddenly floating, floating on the air, hurtled along with the speed of wind, to reach the hut, no longer able to see or breathe.

The door was opened for him.

His hands fumbled at nothing.

The air cleared as the door closed behind him. Yet no one was there to close it.

Only in the middle of the floor stood a handsome fox. He was long legged, lean flanked. His paws were black, his underbelly flushed with cream and the long fur on the rest of his body was a flaunting arrogant copper red, stained with rust. Under his brush the long thick hairs were creamy white. His prick ears were black tipped, his glowing eyes were black rimmed and his stiff whiskers were white.

He bent his front legs and straightened his back legs and invited Johnny to play. To run towards him and to dance with him, ever nearer and nearer to the eye in the corner.

The glowing eye.

The telltale eye.

The scarlet eye of danger.

Danger.

Johnny Toosmall saw the telltale. Saw the red warning, red for blood, red for horror, red for terror, red for fear. Red eyes in the black night.

Press the bell, Johnny.

Sound the alarm Johnny.

Wake the town, Johnny.

Warn the town.

Johnny stumbled on.

His legs were failing him.

He fell forward, his hand seeking the alarm bell as he crashed to the ground.

The siren screamed in the night.

12 Green for Safety

Everyone knew what to do.

Sometimes they played at braving danger.

Now it had come.

Men ran for the fire engines, ran for the ambulances, ran for the gas masks. The police cars swept into the night, sirens screeching.

Run, good people, run.

Gather your belongings.

Leave your homes, make for the moors, empty the houses.

Out, all of you, into the soaking night.

They came fast, aware of panic that fought with sense; mothers nursing babies, holding tiny children by the hand; children crying, unable to understand why they had been torn from their beds, been dressed in a hurry and dragged into the night, dragged into the pouring rain, into the rolling thunder, into the fast fireflicker flashing stormlight.

They came with dogs on leads and cats in baskets, with birds in cages, and with hutches, rabbits and gerbils, hamsters and goldfish, men holding briefcases, a woman with her alarm clock, an old lady gripping a box in which was her cat with its five newborn kittens, a boy holding a tortoise.

A girl, her face creamed, her hair in curlers, holding her vanity set. A bride, only two weeks wed, clutching her wedding dress, an old woman walking slowly, holding the portrait of her dead husband.

Leave your houses.

Hurry, hurry, hurry.

The engines were through the factory gates, but Johnny was not there to greet them. No time for Johnny. Time to put on gas masks and find the leak, find the dead fox and see where the gas seeped out. Shut off the valves. Close the stopcocks.

Work, never mind the risk.

Work.

Forget fear.

Work to save the town. Work to save the factory. Work in the driving rain. Work through the tormented night.

Pray for dawn.

Pray for the lightning to stop.

Pray for silence.

Out on the moors the people knelt and prayed. They sang. They sang to re-assure the children, sang to drown their terror, sang to overcome trembling hands and unnerved legs and the fear of gas.

Praise my soul the King of Heaven....

The words rang out, high and clear, over the sound of the storm.

Alleluia.

Out on the moors the phantom armies marched. The drums soared above the thunder rolls. The people listened fearfully and sang louder, the rumoured haunting real to them for the first time in their lives.

Slowly the thunder growled ever more softly.

The lightning flashes were far apart.

The drums faded.

The dawn brought light; weary men knew that the gas leak was controlled, that the repair was strong, that the poison would blow away.

There was a wind. And there was rain.

Rain and wind, driving from the west; blowing the leafless trees, blowing through a town new cleansed with the dust laid low and the earth packed hard and the rivers beginning to run again.

There was water in the troughs on the farm.

The farmer stood with his wife in the rain and watched the cattle drink. Their coats were free from dust. They moved with vigour.

The farmer knew the fox was dead.

He burned the trap. He would not need it now.

The people returned to their homes.

Johnny Toosmall lay in a hospital bed; a tiny man, his life draining away. He never spoke again. He died next dawn.

Inside the little hut, the green eye glowed bright.

Green for safety. Red for sorrow.

They buried Johnny Toosmall in the churchyard, with the fox lying at his feet. All the town came to his funeral. They picked the tiny wild flowers from the fields, and roses that had been treasured in the gardens.

The days went by. The grass grew green again, the cattle fattened, the rivers filled.

Families slept at night in cool rooms.

Clean breezes blew through the town.

The pestilence died.

There was a new watchman at the factory now. A man Johnny Toosmall had known well, a man newly retired from work, but not yet wanting to live in idleness.

Sometimes, faint and very far away, he thought he heard the throbbing drums; sometimes a small mist crept along the ground; sometimes steel glinted when there was nothing there to catch the light.

Sometimes, soft and mellow, sweet and clear, came the call of a hunting horn.

Sometimes the watchman paused, thinking he saw a man with a dog beside him. A dog with a brushlike tail and glowing eyes. And sometimes in the morning the watchman was surprised to find notes written in the report book in beautiful copperplate.

Six in the morning. The light is green and all is well.

Yet he did not remember writing.

Sometimes, when he was alone, he felt as if another man was standing beside him, offering him companionship and reassurance, and he thought he glimpsed someone who departed without turning his head, a swift moving figure, with a dog beside him. The nightman liked the factory. He liked the air of serenity around him; he enjoyed the feeling of sanctuary when he reached his room; he knew the room welcomed him home.

Sometimes he thought he saw a man sitting there, waiting for him.

He was not sure.

He did not recognize the ghost.

Johnny was six feet tall.

If you would like to receive a newsletter telling you about our new children's books, fill in the coupon with your name and address and send it to:

Gillian Osband,

Transworld Publishers Ltd,

Century House,

61–63 Uxbridge Road, Ealing,

London, W5 5SA

Name ....

Address ....

....

CHILDREN'S NEWSLETTER

All the books on the previous pages are available at your bookshop or can be ordered direct from Transworld Publishers Ltd., Cash Sales Dept. P.O. Box 11, Falmouth, Cornwall.

Please send full name and address together with cheque or postal order—no currency, and allow 40p per book to cover postage and packing (plus 18p each for additional copies).